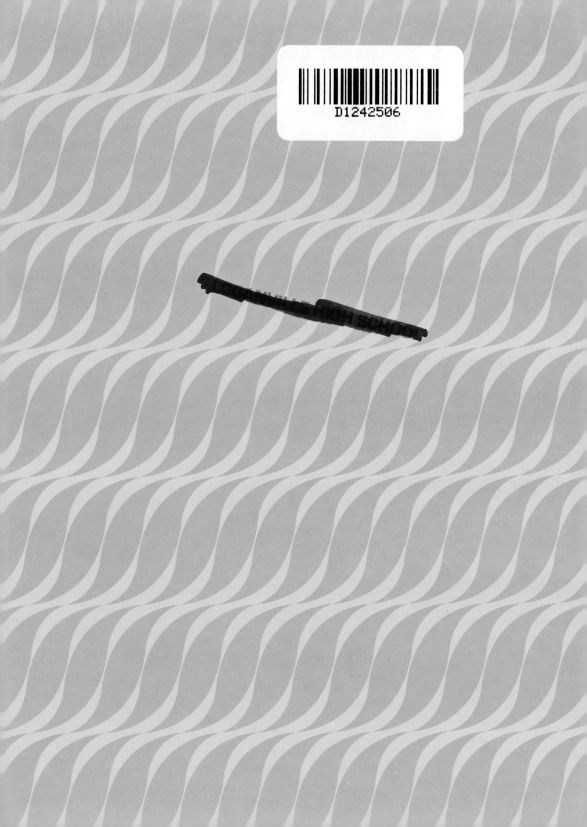

Nature fact file

Ants, Bees
Wasps and Termites

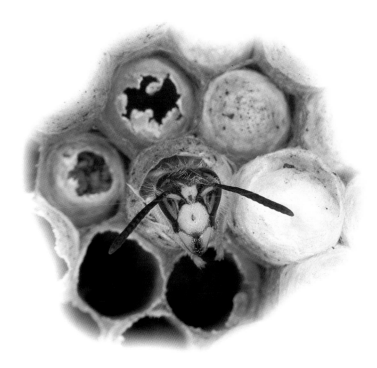

Dr Jen Green
Consultant: Dr. Sarah A Corbet

southwater

C O N

This edition is published by Southwater

Southwater is an imprint of Anness Publishing Ltd
Hermes House, 88–89 Blackfriars Road, London SE1 8HA
tel. 020 7401 2077; fax 020 7633 9499
www.southwaterbooks.com; info@anness.com

© Anness Publishing Ltd 2002, 2004

UK agent: The Manning Partnership Ltd,
6 The Old Dairy, Melcombe Road, Bath BA2 3LR;
tel. 01225 478444; fax 01225 478440;
sales@manning-partnership.co.uk

UK distributor: Grantham Book Services Ltd,
Isaac Newton Way, Alma Park Industrial Estate,
Grantham, Lincs NG31 9SD;
tel. 01476 541080; fax 01476 541061;
orders@gbs-ltd.co.uk

North American agent/distributor: National Book Network,
4501 Forbes Boulevard, Suite 200, Lanham, MD 20706;
tel. 301 459 3366; fax 301 429 5746; www.nbnbooks.com

Australian agent/distributor: Pan Macmillan Australia,
Level 18, St Martins Tower, 31 Market St,
Sydney, NSW 2000;
tel. 1300 135 113; fax 1300 135 103;
customer.service@macmillan.com.au

New Zealand agent/distributor: David Bateman Ltd,
30 Tarndale Grove, Off Bush Road, Albany, Auckland;
tel. (09) 415 7664; fax (09) 415 8892

Publisher: Joanna Lorenz
Managing Editor: Linda Fraser
Project Editors: Rebecca Clunes, Rasha Elsaeed
Copy Editor: Dawn Titmus
Designer: Sarah Williams
Picture Researcher: Su Alexander
Illustrator: Stuart Carter
Production Controller: Claire Rae
Editorial Reader: Jonathan Marshall

Previously published as *Nature Watch: Insect Societies*

10 9 8 7 6 5 4 3 2 1

Ancient Art & Architecture: 4b, 7tr; Anness
Publishing: 4tl, 14tr, 14bl; BBC Natural History
Unit: 11tr, 29br, 55tl, 39tl, 42tr, 42cl, 46cl, 48cl, 50tr,
52bl, 55tl, 56bl, 57tr, 59cr; BBC Wild: 9br, 13br;
Bruce Coleman: 5b, 8c, 17cr, 18br, 21tr, 32bl, 44bl,
50bl, 53tr, 53c; Corbis: 17br, 31bl; Ecoscene: 43cl;
Mary Evans Picture Library: 15bl, 58tl; Heritage
& Natural History Photography: 7c, 23tr, 28br,
30tr, 31c, 35tr, 35cr, 35bl, 36tr, 41cr, 45br, 56tr, 59tr,
59bl, 61cl; Kobal Collection: 23tl; Nature Picture
Library: 29bl; NHPA: 19tr, 21br, 23br, 25cl, 26tl,
29tl, 37tl, 40cl, 40br, 42cr, 49cr, 52cr, 57tl; OSF: 11cl,
12c, 12br, 13tr, 26bl, 26br, 27tl, 27bl, 31tr, 37cr,
38tr, 38cl, 41bl, 43cr, 49bl, 50br, 57cl, 61cr; Papilio:
19bl, 27cr, 29tc; SPL: 6tr, 8tr, 9tl, 16br, 18tr, 20tr,
20bl, 22tr, 24tr, 25cr, 34br, 39tr, 39cl, 45tr, 51cr,
53b, 54tr, 55tl, 55br, 57br, 60tr; Kim Taylor: 6cl,
7bl, 14cr, 17cl, 25tr, 45br, 55tr, 61tl; Warren
Photographic: 4c, 5tl, 5c, 7tl, 9cl, 9cr, 10bl, 10br,
11tl, 11br, 13tl, 13bl, 15br, 16tr, 16bl, 19tl, 21tl, 22cl,
22br, 24cl, 24b, 28tr, 32tl, 32br, 33tl, 35tr, 33bl, 33br,
34tr, 36bl, 36br, 37bl, 58br, 39br, 40tl, 41tl, 44tr,
44cr, 46tr, 46br, 47tr, 47br, 48tr, 48br, 51bl, 52t.

TENTS

What are Social Insects?

Insects are the most successful group of animals on Earth. They make up about three-quarters of all animal species. Most insects have a solitary life, but a few kinds are called social insects because they live and work together in a group known as a colony. Some insect colonies hold hundreds, thousands or even millions of insects. Different members of the colony do different jobs. All ants and termites, some types of bees and a few kinds of wasps are social. For centuries, people have been fascinated by these insects because their colonies seem similar to human societies. Some types of social insects are also important because they make useful products such as honey, and they help to pollinate flowers. For these reasons, social insects are among the world's best-known insect groups.

▲ LONELY LIVES

Most insects, such as these tortoiseshell butterflies, do not live in colonies. They spend almost all of their lives on their own. After mating, the female lays her eggs on a plant that will feed her young when they hatch. Then she flies away, leaving her young to fend for themselves.

▲ ONE LARGE FAMILY

This scene inside a honeybee's nest shows a fertile (breeding) female bee, called the queen, in the center, surrounded by her daughters who are called workers. Social insect colonies are like overgrown families. Each colony is made up of a parent or parents and lots of their offspring, who help bring up more young.

Royal Emblem

This stained-glass window from Gloucester Cathedral, England, shows a fleur-de-lys, the emblem of the French royal family. 'Fleur-de-lys' is a French term for an iris or lily flower. Originally, however, the symbol represented a flying bee with outstretched wings. French kings chose the bee as their symbol because bee colonies function like well-run, hard-working human societies. Bees also represented riches because they made precious honey.

4

◀ TEAMWORK

These weaver ant workers are pulling leaves together to make a nest to protect the colony's young. Like all adult insect workers in a colony, they help rear the young but do not breed themselves. One ant working alone would not be strong enough to pull the leaf together — the task needs a group of ants working as a team.

DIFFERENT JOBS ▶

These two different types of termites are from the same species. The brown insects with large heads and fierce jaws are soldiers. They are guarding the smaller, paler workers, who are repairing damage to the nest. The insects in all social insect colonies are divided into groups called castes. Different castes have different roles, for example worker termites search for food while soldiers guard the nest. In some species, the castes look quite different from each other because they have certain features, such as large jaws, that help them do their work.

◀ NEST BUILDERS

Paper wasps are so-called because they build nests made of chewed wood fibers, or 'paper.' Like these wasps, most social insects live and rear their young inside a nest built by colony members. Some nests, such as those made by some wasps and bees, are complicated, beautiful structures. Some nests, such as those made by certain termites, are huge in size and tower some 20 feet high.

Busy Bees

The insect world contains over a million different species (kinds) of insects. Scientists divide them into large groups called orders. All the insects in an order share certain characteristics. Bees belong to the order Hymenoptera. The name means 'transparent (see-through) wings,' which bees have. Bees are found in most parts of the world except very cold places and tiny ocean islands. Experts have identified 20,000 different bee species. Many types live alone for most of the year, but over 500 species are social. They include honeybees, bumblebees and stingless bees. Honeybees live in colonies larger than those of any other bee.

▲ TINY BEES
This stingless bee is among the world's smallest bees – it is just 1⁄16 inch long. Stingless bees live in hot, tropical countries near the Equator. These bees cannot sting, hence their name.

golden bumblebee
(*Bombus hortorum*)

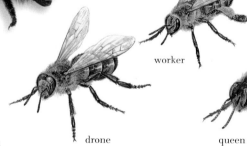

worker

drone

queen

▲ HEAVYWEIGHT INSECT
Bees vary a lot in size. Bumblebees, such as the one shown here, are among the largest species. They grow up to 1½ inches long. Bumblebees are plump, hairy bees found in the Northern Hemisphere in temperate regions. These bees live in small colonies where the queen has just a few workers to help her feed the young bees in the nest.

▲ IDENTITY PARADE
A honeybee colony contains three castes (types) of insect. The queen is the only fertile female. She lays all the eggs, and these hatch into the colony's young. Most of the other bees in the colony are females that do not breed. They are called workers. At certain times of year, male bees, called drones, hatch out. Their role is to mate with the queen so that she will lay more eggs.

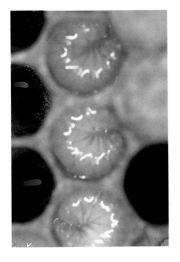

Bees in Ancient Egypt
This Egyptian tomb is carved with symbols of life, one of which is a large bee. The ancient Egyptians were among the first people to keep bees, over 2,500 years ago. They kept honeybees in clay hives, and even moved the hives from place to place in search of nectar-bearing flowers, in the same way some modern beekeepers do. Experts think the bees were probably transported by raft along the Nile River.

▲ SAFE NURSERY

These young honeybees are growing up in the nest, safe inside special cells that the worker bees have constructed. Wild bees usually build their nests in hollow trees or rocky crevices. People rear honeybees in artificial nests called hives, so that they can harvest the bees' honey to eat.

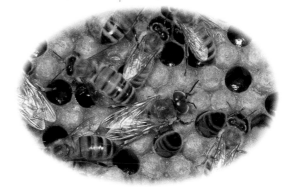

brown bumblebee (*Bombus pascuorum*)

▲ DRONES AND WORKERS

These honeybees are male drones and smaller, female workers. The drones mate with the queen, while worker bees have many different tasks, such as looking after the young, making the nest larger and finding food.

◀ LONG-TONGUED BUMBLEBEE

This brown bumblebee is using her tongue to reach nectar deep inside the flower. Nectar is a sweet liquid made by flowers, which bees feed on. Back in the nest, the nectar is used to make honey. Brown bumblebees can be distinguished from some other bumblebees by their unusually long tongues.

Hard-working Wasps

Bees and wasps are quite closely related. They belong to the same order, Hymenoptera. Like bees, wasps have transparent wings. Wasps live mainly in tropical or temperate regions, although a few species live in cold places. Experts have identified about 17,000 different species of wasps, but only about 1,500 species are social. They include common wasps, hornets and tree wasps. Social wasps live in nests that may contain as many as 5,000 insects. Most wasp nests contain only one fertile female, the queen.

▲ **LARGEST WASPS**
The weight of a queen hornet has caused this flower to drop a petal. European hornets, like the one above, are among the largest wasps, growing up to 1¼ inches long.

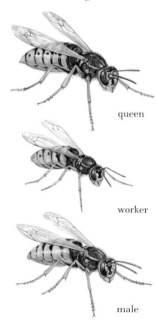

queen

worker

male

▲ **DISTINCTIVE STRIPES**
These common wasp workers are entering their nest hole in a tree. Many types of wasps can be recognized by the bright stripes on their bodies. The colors warn other animals that the wasps are dangerous. Common wasps have yellow and black stripes.

CASTES OF THE COMMON WASP ▶
There are three castes (types) of wasps found in a common wasps' nest – the queen, female workers (her daughters) and males (her sons). The queen is the largest. Male wasps hatch out only in the breeding season.

◄ NEW WORKER

A paper wasp worker looks on as a younger sister, a new worker, hatches from the paper nest cell in which she has developed. Like other social insects, social wasps live in nests containing at least two generations of insects that work together to maintain colony life.

SWEET FEAST ►

Adult wasps like to feed on sweet foods such as fruit, plant sap and flower nectar. In autumn, you will often see common wasp workers gathering to feast on the flesh of ripe apples that have fallen to the ground.

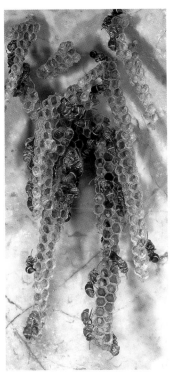

◄ SLENDER NESTS

These Australian paper wasps have attached their nest to the roof of a dark cave. It is sheltered from the weather and from some predators. Some paper wasps build open nests in which the cells are clearly visible, as shown here. Others build a protective cover around their nests.

HOUSEKEEPING ►

This European paper wasp is removing water from her nest after a rainy night. In hot weather, the wasp cools her nest by sprinkling it with drops of water from a stream. Many types of wasps cool their nest by fanning it with their wings. European paper wasps often build open nests that hang from tree trunks.

Amazing Ants

The order Hymenoptera contains ants as well as wasps and bees. However, unlike their cousins, most ants do not have wings. Ants are found in many parts of the world, mostly in hot or warm countries. More than 9,000 different species of ants are found worldwide.

All types of ants are social. Some ant colonies are very large and contain many thousands of individuals. Some ants nest high in trees, but most live underground. Ants are generally small in size. Most are about ⅓ inch long, but some are only ⅟₃₂ inch. Around the world, ants live in many amazing ways. Some species keep certain insects, such as aphids, captive and feed on the sweet food they produce. Other species keep other types of ants as slaves.

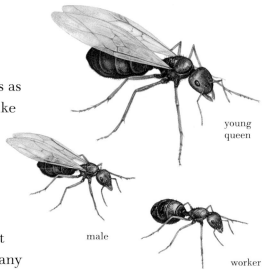

young queen

male

worker

▲ ANT COLONY CASTES

Ant nests contain several different castes (types) of ants. There may be one or several queens, who have plump bodies. Male ants and young queens emerge during the breeding season – at this stage both have wings. Worker ants are smaller than the queen, and they perform many jobs around the nest. Some species of ant have a fourth caste of soldiers, whose job is to defend the colony.

▲ TINY BUT STRONG

This European wood ant is carrying a dead comrade to a garbage dump outside the nest. Ants are very strong for their size. Some species can lift up to 50 times their weight.

FLYING HIGH ▶

Young queens and male ants have wings, and mate in the air. Afterwards, the male ant dies. The queen bites off her wings, as they are no longer needed. She digs into the soil to create a new nest. The queen rears the first brood of workers herself, feeding them on spare eggs and saliva.

▼ A FLYING SAUSAGE

The winged males of African safari ants have rosy, sausage-shaped bodies. They are known as sausage flies. Ants come in many colors, but the commonest colors are red or black.

African safari ant
(*Dorylus helvolus*)

▲ SCARY SOLDIER

An African driver ant soldier readies herself for action. Many species of ants have a special caste of soldiers that have large heads and fierce jaws. The soldiers' job is to protect the colony. African driver ants are particularly fierce. They usually prey on other insects, but sometimes attack much larger creatures, such as birds and lizards, and domestic animals that have been tethered and can't escape. They work together to bring food back to the nest.

▲ SEWING A HOME

Weaver ant workers are holding the pale bodies of young ants, which are spinning silk. Weaver ants make their nests by joining leaves. The workers pull the leaves together, and then sew them with the silken threads.

FIGHT SCENE ▶

Some ants, such as these harvester ants, wage war on those from neighboring colonies to gain possession of a good feeding area. Sometimes, an impressive show of strength is enough to force the rival ants to retreat.

Teeming Termites

Termites belong to the insect order Isoptera. The name means 'equal wings,' even though most termites (the workers) do not have wings. Termites live mainly in tropical countries such as Africa and Australia, although some species are found in temperate parts of North and South America and Europe. All of the 2,000 species of termites are social.

Termites establish the largest insect colonies. A nest may contain up to five million individuals. Unlike other insect societies, a termite colony is made up of roughly equal numbers of males and females. As well as a queen, all termite colonies include a male called the king, who lives with the queen and fertilizes her eggs.

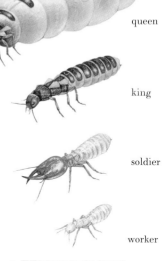

queen

king

soldier

worker

▲ TERMITE CASTES
A termite colony contains four main castes (types) of insect – the queen, king, workers and soldiers. The queen is by far the largest insect in the colony, measuring up to 4 inches long. The workers grow to only ¼ inch, a small fraction of her length.

▼ READY TO BREED
Winged termites emerge from their nest ready for their mating flight. After mating, the new king and queen will found a colony. They shed their wings and will probably remain underground for the rest of their lives.

▲ ROYAL FAMILY
This strange, sausage-shaped object is the termite queen. The rear part of her body is huge because it is swollen with thousands of eggs. Below her, to the right, you can see the king, who is a little larger than the workers in this species. The king and queen normally live in a special chamber deep inside the nest.

▲ PALE INSECTS

This picture shows white, wingless termite workers and fertile (breeding) termites with wings. Most termites are pale in color. For this reason, termites are sometimes called 'white ants,' although they are not closely related to ants. All termite workers and soldiers are blind and wingless.

▲ STRIPY SPECIES

The harvester termite worker has an unusual black-and-cream coloring. Its dark stripes help it to survive as it gathers plant food above the ground. Most termites live underground and find food there. They are pale-colored and often die if exposed to bright sunlight for long.

TALL TOWER ▶

An underground termite mound in Kenya is marked by a tower, which functions as a chimney. It contains ventilation shafts that allow cool air to reach the nest below. The tall spire, made by the tiny insects, may be as high as 25 feet. It is made of moistened mud that later dries rock-hard.

▲ WORKERS AND SOLDIERS

African termite workers gather grass and petals to feed the colony. They are guarded by soldiers, which are large insects with well-armored heads. Both soldier and worker termite castes contain male and female insects – roughly half of each.

Body Parts

Like other insects, adult social insects have six legs. Bees and wasps have wings, but non-breeding ants and termites (workers and soldiers) have no wings. As with other insects, the bodies of social insects are protected by a hard outer case that is called an exoskeleton. This tough covering is waterproof and helps prevent the insect from drying out. An insect's body is divided into three main sections: the head, thorax (middle section) and abdomen (rear).

Social insects differ from non-social insects in some important ways. For example, they possess glands that produce special scents that help them communicate with one another. The various castes also have special features, such as stings.

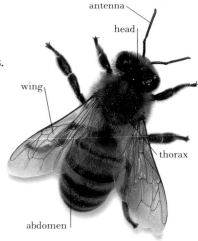

▲ **PARTS OF AN INSECT**
An insect's head holds the main sense organs, including the eyes and antennae. Its wings, if it has any, and legs are attached to the thorax. The abdomen holds the digestive and reproductive parts.

▲ **BEE**
A bumblebee's body is covered with dense hairs. She collects flower pollen in special pollen baskets, surrounded by bristles, on her back legs.

▲ **WASP**
A wasp has narrow, delicate wings and a long body. In many wasp species, the abdomen and thorax are brightly striped.

◄ **ANT**
An ant's abdomen is made up of the petiole (narrow waist) and the gaster (large rear part). The thorax contains strong muscles that move the six legs.

TERMITE ►
Unlike other social insects, termites do not have a narrow waist between their thorax and abdomen. They are less flexible than other social insects.

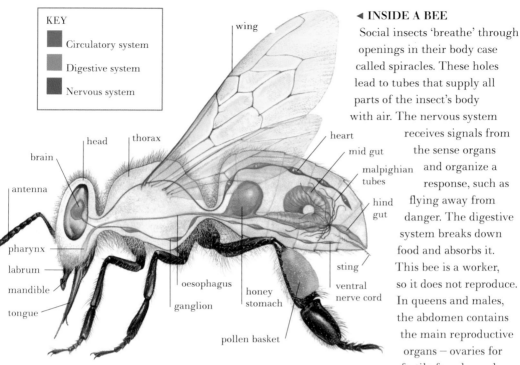

KEY

■ Circulatory system

■ Digestive system

■ Nervous system

wing

head

thorax

brain

antenna

pharynx

labrum

mandible

tongue

oesophagus

ganglion

honey
stomach

pollen basket

heart

mid gut

malpighian
tubes

hind
gut

sting

ventral
nerve cord

◄ INSIDE A BEE

Social insects 'breathe' through openings in their body case called spiracles. These holes lead to tubes that supply all parts of the insect's body with air. The nervous system receives signals from the sense organs and organize a response, such as flying away from danger. The digestive system breaks down food and absorbs it. This bee is a worker, so it does not reproduce. In queens and males, the abdomen contains the main reproductive organs – ovaries for fertile females and testes for males.

Wasp Waist

In the late 19th century, it became fashionable for women to have a narrow 'wasp waist'. Well-to-do ladies achieved this shape by wearing corsets like the one shown in this advertisement. However, the corsets were very tight and pressed on the ribs and lungs. They were very uncomfortable and even caused some women to faint from lack of oxygen.

▲ COLD-BLOODED CREATURES

A queen wasp spends the winter in a sheltered place, such as a woodpile. Like all insects, social insects are cold-blooded, which means that when they are still, their body temperature is the same as the temperature outside. In winter, worker wasps die, but the queen enters a deep sleep called hibernation. She wakes up when the weather gets warmer again in spring.

On the Wing

All adult wasps and bees have two pairs of narrow, transparent wings. They fly to escape their enemies and to get to food that cannot be reached from the ground. Honeybees fly off in swarms (groups) to start a new nest.

The wings of a bee or a wasp are attached to its thorax. Like other flying insects, bees and wasps may bask in the sun to warm their bodies before take-off. They also warm up by exercising their flight muscles. Flying uses up a lot of energy, so bees and wasps eat high-energy foods such as nectar. Most ants and termites are wingless, but young queens and males have wings, which they use during mating.

▲ HOW BEES FLY
Inside the thorax, bees and wasps have two sets of muscles that make their wings move. One set of muscles pulls down on the domed top of the thorax, which makes the wings flip up. Another set pulls on the ends of the thorax, so the top clicks back into its original shape. This makes the wings flip down.

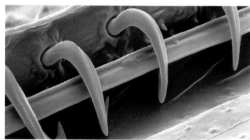

▲ BUZZING BEES
A group of honeybees approaches a flower. Flying bees beat their wings amazingly quickly – at more than 200 beats per second. The beating movement produces a buzzing sound, which becomes more high pitched the faster the wings flap up and down.

▲ HOOKING UP
This row of tiny hooks is on the edge of a bee's front wing. Wasps have wing hooks, too. The hooks attach the front wings to the hind ones when the insect is flying. The large surface area of the combined wings helps the bee fly faster.

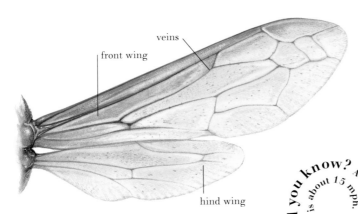

front wing

veins

hind wing

◄ DELICATE WINGS
The front wings of bees and
wasps are bigger than their
hind (back) wings. The
wings are made up of the
same hard material, called
chitin, that covers the rest
of their body, but the wings
are thin and delicate.
They are supported
and strengthened by
a network of veins.

Did you know? A bee's top flying speed is about 15 mph.

French wasp
(*Dolichovespula
media*)

▲ SKILLFUL FLIER
A brown bumblebee hovers in front of a flower.
Bees are very agile in the air. They can move
their wings backward and forward as well
as up and down, so they can fly forward,
reverse and also hover in one place.

▲ KEEPING CLEAN
This queen is cleaning her wings using tiny combs
on her back legs. Bees and wasps clean their
wings regularly to keep them in good working
order. When not in use, they fold their wings
over their backs to protect them from damage.

The Sound of a Bee
*'Flight of the Bumblebee' is a piece of piano music that was written
by the Russian composer Nikolai Andreyevich Rimsky-Korsakov
(1844–1908). The piece was inspired by the buzzing sound that is
made by these flying insects. The fast pace and quavering melody
suggest the buzzing noise made by the bee as she moves from
flower to flower, gathering nectar. The piece is well known for
being very difficult to play.*

Lively Legs

Most ants and termites cannot fly, but they move around and even climb trees using their six legs. Social insects use their legs to groom (clean) their bodies as well.

All insects belong to a larger group of animals called arthropods, which means 'jointed leg'. True to this name, adult insects have many-jointed legs. An insect's legs have four main sections – the coxa, femur, tibia and tarsus. The coxa is the top part of the leg, where it joins to the thorax. The femur corresponds to the thigh, and the tibia is the lower leg. The tarsus, or foot, is made up of several smaller sections. Insects' legs do not have bones. Instead, they are supported by hard outer cases, like hollow tubes.

Did you know? All adult insects have six legs, but young bees, wasps and ants have no legs at all.

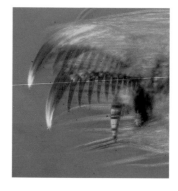

▲ **GRIPPING CLAWS**
This magnified photograph of a bee's foot shows clearly the tiny claws on the end of the foot. Claws help the insects to grip smooth surfaces such as shiny leaves, stems and branches without slipping. Ants can walk along the underside of leaves with the help of their claws.

WALKING ON STILTS ▶
Like other ants, this Australian bulldog ant has legs made up of several long, thin sections. In the hot, dry areas of Australia, the ant's stilt-like legs raise her high above the hot, dusty ground, helping to keep her cool. As well as walking, climbing and running, social insects' legs have other uses. Some ants and termites use their legs to dig underground burrows. Bees carry food using their hind legs.

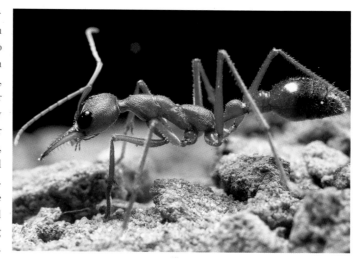

▲ **MULTIPURPOSE LEGS**
Bees use their legs to grip onto flowers and also to walk, carry nesting materials and clean their furry bodies. Their front legs have special notches to clean their antennae. They use their hind legs to carry pollen back to the nest.

▲ **ON THE MOVE**
Army ants spend their whole lives on the move. Instead of building permanent nests as other ants do, they march through the forest in search of prey, attacking any creature they find and scavenging from dead carcasses.

▼ **EXPERT CLIMBERS**
Termites swarm along a tree branch in Malaysia, Southeast Asia. Many termites nest underground, but some build their nests high in trees. They climb vertical surfaces such as trees by digging their claws into the bark.

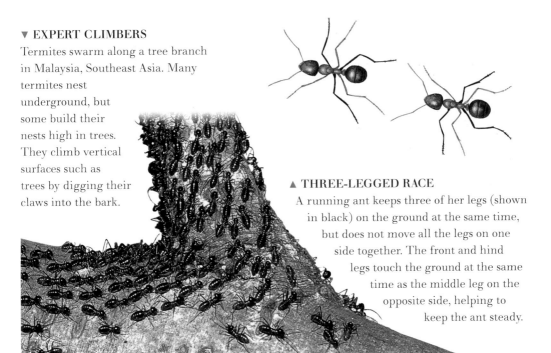

▲ **THREE-LEGGED RACE**
A running ant keeps three of her legs (shown in black) on the ground at the same time, but does not move all the legs on one side together. The front and hind legs touch the ground at the same time as the middle leg on the opposite side, helping to keep the ant steady.

19

Amazing Senses

Social insects find food, escape from danger and communicate with their nestmates with the help of their keen senses. However, the world their senses show them is very different to the one we humans know.

Antennae are the main sense organs for many insects. These long, thin projections on the insect's head are used to smell and feel, and sometimes to taste or hear. Sight is important to wasps, bees and most ants, but many termites have no eyes and are blind. Their world is a pattern of scents and tastes.

Social insects have no ears, so they cannot hear as people do. Instead, they 'hear' using special organs that pick up tiny air currents, or vibrations, produced by sounds. Sensitive hairs all over their bodies help the insects know when danger is near.

▲ **TWO TYPES OF EYE**
This close-up of a wasp shows the large compound eyes that cover much of the head. The curving shape of the eyes allows the wasp to see in front, behind and above at the same time. Compound eyes make out colors and shapes, and are good at detecting movement. On top of the wasp's head are three simple eyes, arranged in a triangle. These detect light and help the wasp know what time of day it is.

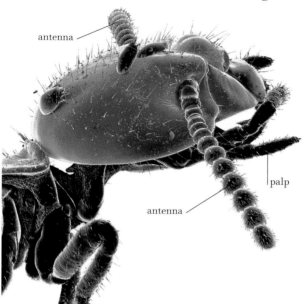

antenna

palp

antenna

◄ **TOUCHY-FEELY**
This close-up of a soldier termite clearly shows its antennae – the main sense organs. They are divided into bead-like segments, which are covered with tiny hair that send signals to the insect's brain. Shorter feelers, called palps, on the mouth give the termite a better sense of touch. The palps help it to find and guide food to its mouth. This termite has tiny parasites called mites crawling on its head.

▲ ELBOW ANTENNAE

A bull ant worker uses her feet to clean her antennae. Ant antennae have a sharp-angled 'elbow' joint, which can be seen here.

▲ BRISTLING WITH SENSES

Honeybee workers have compound eyes, simple eyes and short but sensitive antennae that pick up the scents of flowers. Hairs on the head detect wind speed and tell the bee how fast she is flying.

◄ MANY LENSES

A bee's compound eyes are made up of many small, six-sided lenses. Bees and wasps have thousands of these lenses in each eye. Some ants have only a few. Each lens lies at a slightly different angle to its neighbors on the curved surface of the eye, and each gives a slightly different picture. The insect's brain may combine all these little images to build up a big picture of the world.

human's-eye view

possible bee's-eye view

Did you know? Only the termite king and queen have eyes – workers and soldiers are blind.

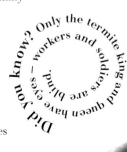

ON THE ALERT ▶

Ants don't have ears, so they use special organs on their antennae, body and feet to 'listen' for prey. This Caribbean ant is lying in wait to pounce on passing small creatures. It is in a special ambush position.

Armed and Deadly

Ants, bees, wasps and termites have many
enemies in the animal kingdom but,
unlike many insects, most social insects
are armed. They use their weapons to
defend the colony, and will often sacrifice their
own lives in so doing. Bees and termites are
armed for defence, but wasps and ants use
their weapons to help kill or capture their prey.

Bees, wasps and some ants are armed with
stings. Some ants and termites have powerful jaws
that can deliver a nasty bite, while others can
squirt a jet of poison at their enemies.
Some wasps and bees have bright
yellow-and-black or red-and-black
markings on their bodies. These
color combinations, known as
warning colors, tell other
creatures that these insects are
dangerous and best avoided.

▲ BARBED SPINES
A worker bee's sting has tiny
barbs on the spine. These catch
in the victim's flesh as the bee
stings, so the bee cannot draw
the sting out again. As the bee
tries to free herself, part of her
abdomen comes away with
the sting, and she dies soon
afterward. Wasps and queen
bees have smooth stings that
they can pull out safely, so they
don't die after they sting.

Did you know? Wasps and bees sting in self defence, so are unlikely to harm you unless you alarm them.

▲ NASTY STINGER
This close-up shows the
sting of a common worker
wasp. The sting of a wasp or
bee consists of a sharp, hollow
spine connected to a venom
(poison) gland in the insect's
abdomen. When the wasp
or bee stings, the spine
punctures its victim's skin,
then the gland pumps venom
into the wound. Only female
wasps and bees have stings.

READY FOR ACTION ▶
Wood ants have powerful jaws
that can give a painful nip.
This cornered worker has taken
up a defensive position with
open jaws ready to bite. Her
abdomen points upward, ready
to spray acid from a poison
gland inside. In this case,
her enemy is probably
the photographer
who is taking
the picture.

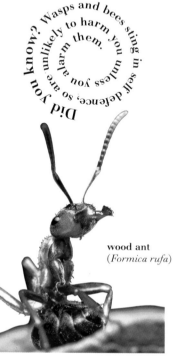

wood ant
(*Formica rufa*)

▲ STINGING BEE

This honeybee is stinging a person's arm. Bee stings cause pain and often produce swelling. If you are stung by a bee, gently ease the sting out, then wash the area with soap and water. A cold, damp cloth can help ease the pain and bring down the swelling. The pain may last only a few minutes, but the swelling may take a day or more to go down.

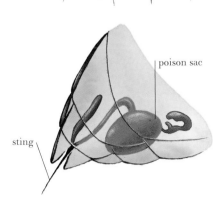

poison sac

sting

▲ INSIDE THE BODY

This diagram shows a wasp's sting, which consists of a smooth, sharp spine attached to a poison gland in its rear end. If you are stung by a wasp, wash the wound with antiseptic. Wasp and bee stings are not life-threatening for people, unless the victim is allergic to stings.

▲ A SOLDIER'S WEAPONS

A leafcutter soldier ant shows off its fierce jaws. Many ants and termites can give their enemies a nasty bite. Some types of termites have long, nozzle-like snouts instead of large jaws. They use the little nozzles to squirt a jet of sticky poison at attackers to kill or immobilize them.

How Insects Eat

The mouthparts of insects are shaped to tackle the particular food they eat. Most social insects eat plant matter, but some species, such as army ants, eat meat and actively hunt their prey. Bees feed on sugary nectar and pollen from flowers. They also use nectar to make honey, which they eat in winter. Bee larvae are fed the same food as adults, but young wasps eat different food. Adult wasps feed mainly on liquid foods, but their larvae eat chewed-up insects.

Many ants eat liquid plant food. Some species lick sweet honeydew from aphids. Other ant species prey on caterpillars and worms, or even lizards, birds and mammals. Most termites and their young eat plant matter. They absorb the goodness in their food with the help of tiny organisms in their guts.

▲ NECTAR COLLECTOR

A honeybee's tongue forms a long, flexible tube that can be shortened or made longer and pointed in any direction. The worker bee uses her tongue like a drinking straw to suck up nectar. She stores most of the liquid in her honey stomach until she returns to the nest.

▲ DUAL-PURPOSE MOUTH

A common wasp laps up juice from an apple. Worker wasps have mouthparts designed to tackle both fluid and insect food. They slurp up liquid food for themselves with their sucking mouthparts, and use their strong jaws to chew up the bodies of insects for the young wasps in the nest.

◄ FEEDING TIME

A honeybee feeds another worker at the nest. As the bee laps flower nectar, strong muscles inside her mouth pump the sweet fluid into her honey stomach. Back at the nest, the worker regurgitates (brings up) the nectar to feed a nestmate, or stores the nectar in special larder cells.

▲ **STRONG-JAWED ANT**

A red carpenter ant shows her large, powerful, toothed jaws, called mandibles. An ant's jaws, which move from side to side, not up and down, are used to break off chunks of plant food.

▲ **DAIRYING ANTS**

These red ant workers are 'milking' black aphids for the sweet liquid called honeydew that the aphids give off as a waste product. Some types of ants keep the aphids like miniature cattle. They 'milk' their captives by stroking them with their antennae to get them to release the honeydew. The ants protect the aphids from their enemies, and, in return, have a ready supply of food.

◄ **WOOD-MUNCHERS**

Termites feed mainly on soft, decaying wood in fallen trees and in human settlements. In tropical countries, they can damage wooden houses and destroy furniture, books and other wood products. They also cause great damage in farm fields and orchards if they infest trees or crops.

HELP WITH DIGESTION ►

Inside a termite's body live even smaller creatures. These strange, pear-shaped forms are called protozoans and they live inside the guts of termites. This photo was taken using a microscope and has been magnified 65 times. Inside the termite's gut, the protozoans digest cellulose, a tough material that forms the solid framework of plants. In this way, the protozoans, and other tiny organisms called bacteria, help termites to break down and absorb the goodness in their food.

The Gardens of the

Leafcutter ants from Central and South America have rather unusual feeding habits. They live in underground nests where they grow their own food – a type of fungus (like tiny mushrooms). This particular fungus is found only in the ants' nests. The leafcutters tend them carefully in special chambers called fungus gardens. Leafcutter ants feed their fungi on bits of leaves that they snip from plants near the nest.

1 Leafcutter ants are so called because they snip off pieces of leaves with their sharp, pointed jaws. They use the leaf pieces to grow the special fungus that forms the ants' food. A huge quantity of vegetation is needed to keep the leafcutters' fungus gardens well supplied.

A leafcutter nest contains several types of workers that do different tasks. Some workers maintain the nest and feed and care for the queen and young, just as in most colonies. Other workers snip leaves and carry them back to the nest. Gardener ants prepare the leaf food for the fungi.

2 A line of leafcutter ants hoists the snipped leaves above their heads to carry them back to the nest. Leafcutter ants are also called parasol ants because the snipped leaves look like tiny parasols, or sunshades. The line of ants forms a small but spectacular parade as it makes its way back to the nest.

3 These leafcutter ant workers are large and strong enough to carry pieces of leaf many times their own size in their mandibles (jaws). In some leafcutter ant species, tiny ants called minors ride on the snipped leaves. They guard their larger worker sisters from flies that try to lay their eggs on the busy workers.

Leafcutter Ants

4 A line of leaf-carrying ants reaches the nest hole. There the leaf-bearers drop their loads for the gardener ants to deal with, and go back for more leaves. If heavy rain starts to fall, the ants drop their leaves and hurry to the nest site. Experts think they do this because a batch of soaking leaves would upset conditions inside the nest, and perhaps damage the growing fungi.

5 Gardener ants carefully tend the patches of fungi so that they will flourish. They snip up the leaves into smaller pieces and chew them up to form a compost for the fungi to grow in. They fertilize the compost with their droppings, and spread special chemicals to kill bacteria that might harm the fungi. Other workers remove debris from the fungus gardens and keep them clean.

6 All leafcutter ants, including the queen (who is shown here) and her young, feed exclusively on the fungi. When a young queen leaves the nest to start a new colony, she carries a piece of fungus in her mouth, which she plants in her new nest. If the new colony flourishes, it may one day hold a million workers. A large colony of leafcutter ant workers may shift up to 40 tons of soil as they excavate their vast underground nest.

Social Insect Habitats

Huge numbers of social insects live in tropical regions, where the climate is hot all year round. They include most termites and many different types of ants, wasps and bees. Rainforests are home to a greater variety of insects, including social species, than any other habitat on Earth. Many termite species live in dry grasslands, or savannas. Scrublands on the edges of deserts are home to some hardy social insects, such as honeypot ants. The world's temperate regions have warm summers and mild or coolish winters. They provide many different habitats, which are home to particular kinds of social insects. The polar regions are generally too cold for insects to survive.

▲ FOREST BIVOUAC
Driver ants spend their lives on the move through the South American rainforests. At night, the workers lock claws and form a ball, called a bivouac, to make a living nest.

◄ LIVING CUPBOARD
Honeypot ants live in dry parts of the world, including the southwestern United States, Mexico and Australia. During the rainy season, the ants gather nectar. They store the sweet food in the crops (honey stomachs) of ants called repletes, whose bodies swell to form living honeypots. The repletes hang from the roof of the nest and feed the other ants during the dry season.

KEEPING COOL AND DRY ►
Some African termites nest in tropical forests where rain falls almost every day. These species build broad caps on their ventilation chimneys to prevent rain dripping into the nest. The chimneys provide a vital cooling system. Being wingless, termites cannot keep their nests cool by fanning them with their wings, as tropical wasps and bees do.

◄ TREETOP TERRITORY

These ants are making a nest by binding leaves together with silk. Some tree-dwelling ants establish large treetop territories that include many nests. African weaver ant colonies, for instance, can contain up to 150 nests in 20 different trees. The ants patrol a territory of 1,600 sq yards — one of the largest insect territories ever known.

PINEFOREST HOME ►

A wasp queen perches on her home. In rainy parts of the world, wasps' nests with open cells are constructed with the cells sloping downward, so rainwater can't collect in them. Other species build an outer covering around the nest to protect the young wasps from the elements.

▲ MOUNTAIN-DWELLER

Bumblebees live mainly in northern temperate regions where the climate is coolish. They also live in mountainous parts of the tropics, where the height of the land keeps the air cool. In winter, the queen hibernates in a burrow, where the temperature is warmer than above ground. Her thick coat helps her to keep warm.

▲ HONEYBEES IN THE RAIN

Honeybees normally shelter on the comb inside the hive or nest cavity in rainy weather and do not venture outside to forage. If the comb becomes exposed to the elements for any reason, the bees will adopt a heads-up position when it rains, so the water drains off their bodies.

Bee and Wasp Nests

Social bees and wasps build complex nests that house the queen, workers and young. Some of these insects nest underground, but many make their homes high in trees or caves, or under the eaves of houses.

Bee and wasp nests contain small six-sided brood cells where the young are reared. Some species also use the cells to store food. These little cells are often built in flattish sheets called combs. In warm countries, wasps and bees often build open-celled nests with no protective covering. In cooler countries, many species protect their nest by enclosing it in a tough covering. In the wild, honeybees construct nests with long, slender open-celled combs. They also live in human-made hives. Bumblebees live in smaller nests, often underground. Some tropical wasps build heavy mud nests hanging from a tree branch. These nests have a long, vertical, slit-shaped opening.

▲ **HOME SWEET HOME**
Wild honeybees nest in tree holes. The slender combs are covered with cells made from wax. Workers have special glands on the underside of their abdomens to produce the wax.

HIDDEN NEST ▶
Bumblebee queens make homes in abandoned animal burrows, rocky crevices or grassy hollows. The small nest contains an untidy comb with a few brood cells for the young. The queen also builds a little pot to store honey, which she feeds on in spring when she incubates her first batch of eggs. Bumblebee workers die off in winter, and only the young queens survive.

◀ BELL-SHAPED HOME

In Venezuela in South America, these tropical wasps have built a bell-shaped nest hanging from a tree branch. The nest looks heavy, but it is made of chewed wood fibers, and so is in fact fairly light.

▲ OUT OF HARM'S WAY

This long, slender wasps' nest in Central America is out of the reach of many enemies. The nest is protected by a heavy paper cover and has a small opening at the bottom. When threatened, some tropical wasps beat their wings on the nest cover to make a loud sound that frightens enemies away.

CAMOUFLAGED AS A TWIG ▶

In South America, some species of wasps build long, thin nests that resemble slender twigs hanging downward, such as this one from Peru. Other South American wasps construct a paper nest with more prickles than a porcupine. Around the world, wasp nests vary in size as well as shape. The smallest are tiny, and the largest measure up to 3 feet long.

◀ NEST WITHIN A NEST

This skillful weaver bird in southern Africa is making its nest by tying grass into knots. The nest is hanging from a branch. Sometimes, a colony of African wasps will build their own home inside a weaver bird's nest. The wasps' brood cells are protected from the weather. In return, the stinging insects help protect the birds from their enemies.

31

Building a

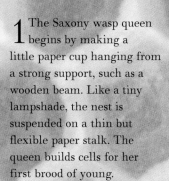

A Saxony wasp nest is started by the queen alone, without any help from her workers. The nest is made from chewed-up wood fibers. It begins as a tiny cup and gradually grows to the size of a football or even larger. The gnawed fibers are soft and flexible at first, but later dry hard and tough. While the nest is still small, the queen lays an egg in each cell on the comb. When the larvae (young insects) hatch, she feeds them on chewed-up insects. When her first brood become adult workers, they take over the day-to-day running of the colony. As the numbers of insects in the colony grow, the nest gets bigger.

1 The Saxony wasp queen begins by making a little paper cup hanging from a strong support, such as a wooden beam. Like a tiny lampshade, the nest is suspended on a thin but flexible paper stalk. The queen builds cells for her first brood of young.

2 The queen collects fibers for her nest from an old fence post. She scrapes away small slivers of wood with her jaws, leaving little telltale grooves in the post. The rasping sound she makes with her jaws can be heard from some distance away. She has to make many trips to collect enough paper for the nest.

3 At night, the wasp queen sleeps coiled around the stem of her nest. You can see the brood cells hanging down inside the cup. Soon the queen will lay a tiny egg at the bottom of each cell. She glues the eggs firmly so they do not drop out.

Saxony Wasp Nest

4 The queen builds a second paper 'envelope' around her nest to strengthen it. As the sides of the cup are extended downward, the nest becomes more rounded. Eventually, only a small entry hole is left at the bottom so the wasps can enter and leave. Having a small opening makes the nest easier to defend.

5 When the worker wasps emerge, they take over many tasks around the nest, including enlarging the nest. These workers are feeding the next batch of young. You can see the pale larvae curled up inside the open cells. Freed of her other duties, the queen is able to concentrate on laying eggs.

6 A worker improves the nest by adding a new layer to the outer covering. Inside, the old layers of envelope are gnawed away to make room for more brood cells. Toward the end of the season, young queens and male wasps hatch out and fly off to find mates. The queens will start new colonies the following year.

7 This abandoned Saxony wasp nest has been cut in half so you can see inside. The fully developed nest is the size of a football. Like a multistory building, it contains many 'floors' of cells that are supported by paper pillars and connected by vertical passageways.

33

Ant and Termite Homes

Nests built by ants and termites come in many different shapes and sizes. Most build their colonies underground, but others live high in trees. Some ants' nests are tiny and contain only a small number of insects. They may be small enough to fit in tiny hollows in twigs or even inside the thorns of spiky plants. Other species live in vast underground colonies that shelter millions of workers and may cover an area the size of a tennis court.

Termites are master builders. Some species build vast underground homes with tall towers above ground that act as ventilation chimneys. These amazing structures allow cool air to flow through the living quarters of the colony, which keeps conditions comfortable there.

Did you know? Termites can control the temperature inside their nest to within ½°F.

▲ **COSY FOREST HOME**
In European woodlands, wood ants build large, domed nests of soil, twigs and pine needles. There may be a dozen separate mounds linked by a network of tunnels. In winter, the ants retreat to the deepest, warmest part of the nest. They move back into the upper chambers when the weather warms up again in spring.

◄ **INSIDE AN ANTS' NEST**
An ants' nest is a maze of narrow tunnels leading to wider living spaces called rooms or chambers. The queen lives and lays her eggs in a large chamber. The young ants are fed and reared in separate rooms called nurseries. Worker ants rest and gather in their own quarters. Other rooms are for storage of food, or garbage dumps.

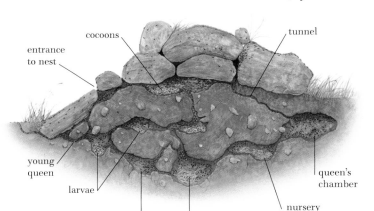

cocoons

tunnel

entrance to nest

young queen

larvae

male ants

worker ants' chamber

nursery for the young

queen's chamber

◀ A TERMITE PALACE

African termites live in an elaborate, domed nest. The soil mound includes a royal chamber for the queen and king, and nurseries for the young. It also contains fungus gardens where the insects grow their own food using methods similar to those of leafcutter ants.

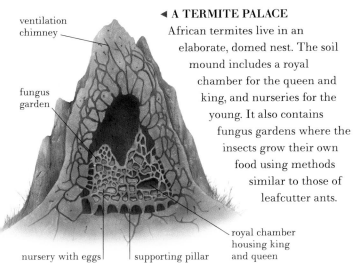

ventilation chimney

fungus garden

nursery with eggs

supporting pillar

royal chamber housing king and queen

▲ MUSHROOM CAP

Some termites from West Africa build mushroom-shaped mud chimneys. The shape helps the rain to run off easily. This chimney has been cut in half so you can see inside. It is full of tiny passages that the workers can open or block to adjust the temperature in the nest below. Up to five mushroom caps are sometimes stacked on top of one another.

TREE HOUSE ▶

Most termites nest underground, but some species build treetop nests, such as this one in eastern Mexico. Nests on the ground are built of mud or sand. Tree nests are usually made from wood fibers moistened with the insects' saliva — a mixture that dries as hard as rock.

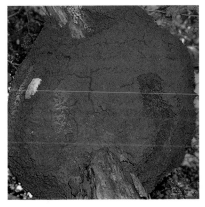

◀ USING THE SUN

Australian compass termites are so-called because they build nests with unusual, flat-sided chimneys that all face in the same direction, east–west. This allows the nest to be warmed by the weak rays of the sun at dawn and dusk. Only the narrow face of the chimney faces the fierce midday sun, which helps keep the nest cool.

Bee and Wasp Colonies

Social bee and wasp colonies work like miniature, smooth-running cities. Like good citizens, all the insects in the colony instinctively know their roles and carry out their tasks.

In a honeybee colony, the workers perform different tasks according to their age. The youngest workers stay in the nest and spend their first weeks cleaning out the brood cells. Later they feed the young. As the wax glands in their abdomen develop, they help build new cells. They also keep the nest at the right temperature. After about three weeks, the worker honeybees go outside to fetch nectar and pollen to store or to feed their sisters. The oldest, most-experienced workers act as guards and scouts. Many wasp colonies work in a similar way, with workers doing different jobs according to their age.

▲ **ADJUSTING THE HEAT**
Honeybees are very sensitive to tiny changes in temperature. The worker bees adjust the temperature around the brood cells to keep the air at a constant 90°F. In cold weather, they cluster together to keep the brood cells warm. In hot weather, they spread out to create cooling air channels.

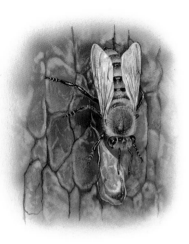

◄ **NEST REPAIRS**
Worker honeybees use a sticky tree resin to repair cracks in their nest. This gummy material is also known as propolis, or 'bee glue.' The bees carry it back to the nest in the pollen baskets on their hind legs. If there is no resin around, the bees may use tar from roads instead.

▲ **BUILDING NEW CELLS**
Honeybee cells are made by workers using wax from their abdomens. The bees use their antennae to check the dimensions of the cells because they must be the right size to fit the young.

◀ THREAT DISPLAY
Paper wasp workers from Equador in South America swarm over the outside of their nest to frighten off intruders. Like all wasp workers, one of their main roles is to defend the nest. If this display fails, the wasps will attack and sting their enemy. However, most animals will retreat as quickly as they can.

▲ PRECIOUS CARGO
A worker honeybee unloads her cargo of nectar. The bees use the nectar to make honey, which is a high-energy food. The honeybee workers eat the honey, which allows them to survive long, cold winters in temperate regions, when other worker bees and wasps die.

TENDING THE YOUNG ▶
A honeybee tends the larvae (young bees) in the nest cells. Honeybees feed their young on nectar and pollen from flowers. Wasp workers feed their larvae on balls of chewed-up insects. The young sister is allowed to feed for about ten seconds, then the worker remolds the food ball and offers it to another larva. The adult may suck juices from the insect meat before offering it to the young. Up to four larvae can feed on the ball.

◀ LITTLE BUMBLEBEE NESTS
Social bumblebees, shown here, live in much smaller colonies than honeybees. European bumblebee nests usually hold 20–150 insects, whereas a thriving honeybee colony may hold 60–80,000 insects. The queen bumblebee helps her workers with the day-to-day running of the nest as well as laying eggs.

37

Ant and Termite Societies

Like bee and wasp societies, ant colonies are all-female for much of the year. Males appear only in the breeding season to mate with the young queens. Ant colonies are tended by hundreds or thousands of sterile female workers. The worker ants also fight off enemies when danger threatens, repair and expand the nest, and adjust conditions there. Some ants use the workers from other species as 'slaves' to carry out these chores.

In most types of ants, the large queen is still nimble and active. However, the termite queen develops a huge body and becomes immobile. She relies on her workers to feed and care for her, while she produces masses of eggs.

▲ ON GUARD

These ants are guarding the cocoons of queens and workers, who will soon emerge. One of the workers' main tasks is to defend the colony. If you disturb an ants' nest, the workers will rush out with the cocoons of young ants and carry them to a new, safe site.

▼ RIVER OF ANTS

Safari ants march through the forest in long lines called columns. The workers, carrying the cocoons of young ants, travel in the middle of the column, where it is safer. They are flanked by a line of soldiers on each side. Resembling a river of tiny bodies, the column may stretch more than 100 yards.

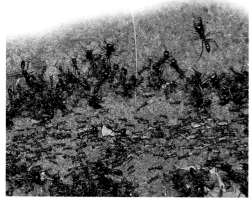

▲ ANT RAIDERS

Slavemaker ants survive by raiding. Here an ant is carrying off a worker from another species. Some slavemakers, such as red Amazon ants, have sharp, pointed jaws that are good for fighting, but no use for other tasks. They rely on ant slaves to gather food and run the nest.

◄ TERMITE SKYSCRAPER

These African termite workers are building a new ventilation chimney for their nest. African termites build the tallest towers of any species, up to 25 feet high. If humans were to build a structure of the same height relative to our body size, we would have to build skyscrapers that were more than 6 miles high. The tallest skyscraper today is less than 1,650 feet tall.

FAMILY LIFE ►

A queen termite is flanked by the king (the large insect below her), workers and young termites. The king and queen live much longer than the workers – for 15 years or even more in some species. The queen may lay 30,000 eggs in a day – that is one every few seconds. The king stays at her side in the royal chamber and fertilizes all the eggs.

Did you know? A column of army ants on the march may contain 150,000 insects.

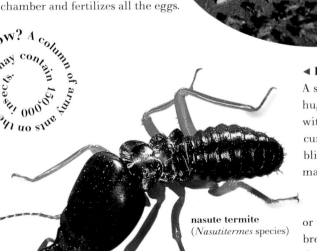

nasute termite
(*Nasutitermes* species)

◄ BLIND GUARD

A soldier termite displays its huge head, which is packed with muscles to move the curved jaws at the front. Being blind, the guard detects danger mainly through scent, taste and touch. Like termite workers, soldiers may be either male or female, but they do not breed. The arch-enemies of these plant-eating insects are meat-eating ants, which hunt them for food.

39

How Social Insects

THE QUEEN'S SCENT
Honeybee workers lick and stroke their queen to pick up her pheromones. If the queen is removed from the nest, her supply of pheromones stops. The workers rear new queens who will produce the vital scents.

Communication is the key to the smooth running of social insect colonies. Colony members interact using smell, taste, touch and sound. Social insects that can see also communicate through sight. Powerful scents called pheromones are the most important means of passing on information. These strong smells, given off by special glands, are used to send a wide range of messages that influence nestmates' behavior. Workers release an alarm pheromone to rally their comrades to defend the colony. Ground-dwelling ants and termites smear a scent on the ground to mark the trail to food. Queens give off pheromones that tell the workers she is alive and well.

TERMITE PHEROMONES
A queen termite spends her life surrounded by workers who are attracted by her pheromones. The scents she releases cause her workers to fetch food, tend the young and enlarge or clean the nest.

FRIEND OR FOE?
Two black ants meet outside the nest and touch antennae to identify one another. They are checking for the particular scent given off by all colony members. Ants with the correct scent are greeted as nestmates. 'Foreign' ants will probably be attacked.

Communicate

THIS WAY, PLEASE

A honeybee worker exposes a scent gland in her abdomen to release a special scent that rallies her fellow workers. The scent from this gland, called the Nasonov gland, is used to mark sources of water. It is also used like a homing beacon to guide other bees during swarming, when the insects fly in search of a new nest.

ALARM CALL

These honeybees have come to the hive entrance to confront an enemy. When alarmed, honeybees acting as guards give off an alarm pheromone that smells like bananas. The scent tells the other bees to come to the aid of the guards against an enemy. In dangerous 'killer bee' species, the alarm pheromone prompts all hive members to attack, not just those guarding the nest.

SCENT TRAIL

This wood ant worker has captured a worm. The ant is probably strong enough to drag this small, helpless victim back to the nest herself. A worker that comes across larger prey returns to the nest to fetch her comrades, rubbing her abdomen along the ground to leave a scent trail as she does so. Her fellow workers simply follow the smelly trail to find the food. Ants can convey as many as 50 different messages by releasing pheromones and through other body language.

The Search for Food

Social insects work in teams to bring back food
for the colony. Experienced workers acting as
scouts search for new food sources. When
they are successful, they return to the nest
and communicate their information to their
comrades. The workers are then able to
visit the same food source. Ants mark the trail
to the food with pheromones.

Bees and wasps fly back to the nest with their
food. Some ants carry food to the nest in long
lines, guarded by soldiers. They may need to cut
up the food into manageable pieces, or work
together to lift heavy loads. Worker
wasps feed their young on chewed-
up insects. In return,
the larvae produce
a sweet saliva
that the adults
feed on.

▲ STORING BUDS
These harvester ants live in the
Sonoran Desert in the western
United States. They take seeds
and buds to the nest to store
in chambers called granaries.
Ants that live in dry places put
food aside for the times when
there is nothing to eat.

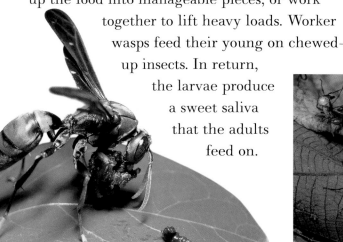

▲ MAKING MEATBALLS
A wasp converts her caterpillar prey to a ball
of pulp, which will be easier to carry back to
the nest. Social wasps kill their insect prey by
stinging them or simply chewing them to
death. The wasp then finds a safe perch and
cuts off hard parts such as the wings. She
chews the rest of the body into a moist ball.

▲ LARGE PRIZE
This column of Central American army ants
has captured a katydid, a type of grasshopper.
Soldiers hold down the struggling insect while
a group of workers arrives to cut it into pieces.
Army ants spend most of their lives on the
move, but sometimes stay in one place while
the colony's newly hatched young grow up.

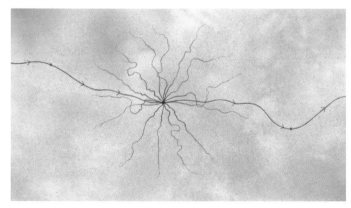

◄ RAIDING PATTERN

This diagram shows the temporary camp of a colony of army ants. When camping, a column of ants marches out to raid for food. Each day, the ants take a different direction, which varies about 120 degrees from the route of the previous day. Their routes form a star pattern radiating from the nest. Army ants camp for about three weeks.

▼ AN ARMY OF TERROR

Army ants are feared forest hunters. They mainly hunt small creatures, such as this insect, but will also kill large animals such as dogs, goats and even horses that are tied up and unable to escape.

▲ KEPT IN THE DARK

Termites scurry along a hidden highway they have built inside a fallen log. These insects forage widely in search of food, but seldom move into the open because bright sunlight harms them. Instead, they excavate long tunnels by digging through soft wood or earth. When moving above ground, they roof over their highways with moistened soil.

SWEET FOOD ►

A European hornet sucks nectar from a hogweed flower. This sweet liquid forms a staple food for both adult bees and wasps. The young wasps produce a sweet saliva that the adult workers also feed on. In autumn, no more eggs are laid, so the supply of saliva stops. Deprived of this food, the wasp workers wander in search of other sweet fluids to drink, such as fruit sap.

43

Bees and Flowers

Flowering plants provide bees with nectar and pollen. In turn, many plants depend on the bees to reproduce. In order to make seeds, plants must be fertilized by pollen from the same species. This process is known as pollination. Many plants are pollinated by nectar-gathering insects such as honeybees. As the bee wanders over a flower collecting food, the pollen grains stick to her hairy body. When she visits a second flower, the grains rub off to pollinate the second plant. Plants that are fertilized in this way produce flowers with bright colors, sweet scents and special shapes to attract the insects.

Back at the nest, the pollen and nectar are fed to the other bees or stored in larder cells. The nectar is concentrated and matures to make honey. Bee scouts tell other workers about sites with many flowers by performing a special dance.

▲ WHERE THE BEE SUCKS
A white-tailed bumblebee approaches a foxglove, attracted by its tall spike of bright flowers. The plant's bell-shaped flowers are just the right size for the bee to enter.

▲ BUSY AS A BEE
A white-tailed bumblebee worker feeds from a thistle. If the weather is good, a bee may visit up to 10,000 flowers in a single day.

◄ HONEY TUMMY
A honeybee sucks up nectar with her long tongue and stores it in her honey stomach. She may visit up to 1,000 flowers before her honey stomach is full and she returns to the nest.

GUIDING LIGHT ►

In ultraviolet light, dark lines or markings show up on flowers such as this potentilla. Called nectar guides, the markings radiate out from the centers of flowers, which often contain nectar. The markings are very noticeable to bees, who can see ultraviolet light. They guide the insect to the flower's center, where she can gather food.

Did you know? A large honeybee colony eats 560 pounds of honey in a year.

circular dance   figure-eight dance

◄ BEE DANCES

Honeybees perform a dance to tell their nestmates where nectar-producing flowers are. When the flowers are close, the bee performs a circular dance on the comb, first in one direction, then in the other. If the food is far way, the bee performs a figure-eight dance, waggling her abdomen as she reaches the middle of the figure. The angle between the line of waggles and the vertical is the same as the angle between the sun, the hive and the food.

ROBBER BEE ►

A honeybee gathers nectar from a runner bean flower. Not all bee visits help plants to reproduce. Some bees gather nectar by biting a hole in the base of the flower so the insect avoids being dusted with pollen. The bee gets her food, but far from helping the plant with pollination, she damages the flower. This process is known as robbing. This honeybee is re-using a hole made by a bumblebee.

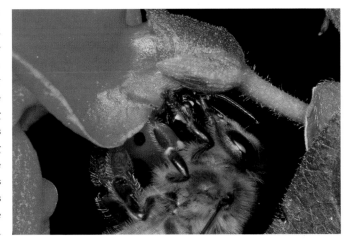

45

Life Cycle of Bees and Wasps

There are four different stages in the life cycle of bees and wasps. They start life as eggs, and hatch into worm-like larvae (grubs). Each larva is fed by the workers, so it does not need legs to move about and find food. When fully grown, the larva enters a resting stage and is called a pupa. Sealed inside its cell, the larva's body breaks down into mush and is reformed into an adult bee or wasp. Finally, the fully formed adult breaks out of its cell. This process is called complete metamorphosis.

For much of the year, only sterile (non-breeding) worker wasps and bees develop. During the breeding season, male insects and young queens are reared. Some bees fly off and mate high in the air. The queens store sperm (male sex cells) in their abdomen. The males die soon after, but the young queens live on and begin to lay eggs.

▲ **FROM EGG TO LARVAE**
Honeybees begin life as pale, pin-sized eggs, like the ones seen here on the right. The eggs hatch and grow into fat, shiny grubs, seen here coiled in their cells. Like all bees and wasps, the queen controls the sex of the grubs. If she fertilises the egg with sperm, it develops into a female (and becomes either a queen or a worker). Unfertilized eggs develop into male drones.

HONEYBEE PUPA ▶
This pale form is a honeybee pupa. Inside the transparent case, the insect has developed legs, wings, eyes, antennae and all the other adult body parts. The young bee will soon emerge. In honeybees, the queens, drones and workers take different amounts of time to develop. Workers take 21 days, drones take 24, while queens develop in only 16 days.

▲ **MATING WASPS**
A male wasp courts a queen by stroking her with his antennae and rubbing his abdomen on hers. Soon the insects will mate. In temperate regions, male wasps and young queens emerge in late summer, then fly away from the nest and find mates.

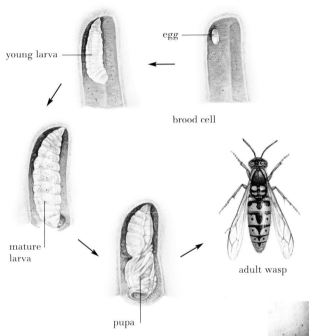

SWARM SCOUTS ▶

Bees start new colonies by swarming, as shown here. The queen leaves the nest with half her workers in a swarm (group), leaving the nest to a young fertilized queen. The swarming bees gather in a buzzing ball on a tree branch, while scouts, in the foreground, fly off to find a new nest site. They return and perform a dance to tell the other bees where the new site is. Then the swarm flies there and builds the new nest.

young larva

egg

brood cell

mature larva

pupa

adult wasp

◀ FROM EGG TO WORKER

This diagram shows the life cycle of a wasp. The queen lays a tiny egg at the bottom of each brood cell, which hatches out into a legless grub. The grub is fed by the queen or the workers on a rich diet of chewed insects, and grows quickly. When fully grown, the larva pupates to emerge as an adult wasp.

BIRTH OF A WASP ▶

A young tree wasp emerges from its brood cell, transformed from larva to adult. It breaks through the silken cap that it spun to close the cell before becoming a pupa. (Bee cells are sealed with wax by the workers.) This cell will soon be cleaned by a worker so another egg can be laid inside. Wasps take between 7 and 20 days to grow from egg to adult, depending on their species and the climate.

Young Ants and Termites

Like wasps and bees, ants have a four-stage life cycle. From eggs, they hatch into legless grubs. When they are large enough, they become pupae, and then adults.

For most of the year, the ant colony rears only sterile workers, but during the breeding season, fertile males and females appear. Unlike other ants, these have wings. During her mating flight, a queen receives a store of sperm, which will fertilize all the eggs she will lay in her lifetime.

Termites have a different life cycle, with only three stages. From eggs, they hatch into young called nymphs, which look like the adults but are smaller. The nymphs feed and grow and gradually reach full size.

▲ BABYSITTING DUTY
Black ant workers tend the colony's young – the small, transparent grubs and large, pale, sausage-shaped pupae. Workers feed the grubs for a few weeks until they are ready to become pupae. Some ant larvae spin themselves a protective silk cocoon before pupating. They emerge as adults after a few weeks.

▲ MOVING THE BROOD
Weaver ant workers in an African forest have assembled the colony's eggs, grubs and pupae on a leaf before carrying them to a new site. The larvae produce silk, which the workers will use to create a new, leafy nest-ball.

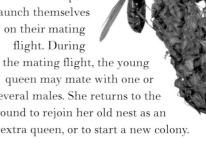

UP AND AWAY ▶
A group of young black ant queens launch themselves on their mating flight. During the mating flight, the young queen may mate with one or several males. She returns to the ground to rejoin her old nest as an extra queen, or to start a new colony.

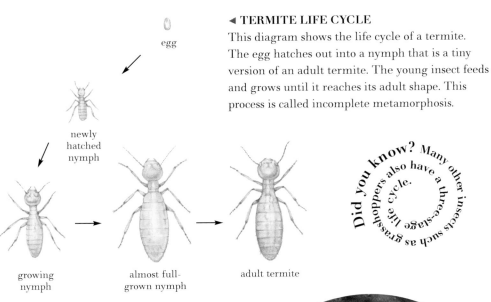

egg

newly
hatched
nymph

growing
nymph

almost full-
grown nymph

adult termite

◄ TERMITE LIFE CYCLE

This diagram shows the life cycle of a termite.
The egg hatches out into a nymph that is a tiny
version of an adult termite. The young insect feeds
and grows until it reaches its adult shape. This
process is called incomplete metamorphosis.

Did you know? Many other insects such as grasshoppers also have a three-stage life cycle.

TERMITE DEVELOPMENT ►

For a long time, experts thought that
termite castes were determined during
reproduction, and that workers and soldiers
were naturally sterile. Recently it has been
discovered that the insects absorb chemicals
from the queen in their food that prevent
them from becoming fertile. If the king
and queen die, nymphs at a particular stage
in their growing cycle develop reproductive
organs and become new kings or queens.

◄ FOUNDERS OF A NEW COLONY

Winged, fertile male and female termites,
shown here, develop in termite colonies
during the breeding season. They have
harder, darker bodies than other termites,
and compound eyes so they can see. These
fertile insects fly off and pair up to start new
colonies. They shed their wings, but the male
does not die as in other types of social insects.
He stays with the queen and fertilizes her
eggs to father all the insects in the colony.

49

Insect Enemies

Bees, wasps, ants and termites provide a rich source of food for many animal predators, ranging from large mammals to birds, lizards, frogs, toads and small creatures. A bees' nest, in particular, contains a feast of different foods – stored honey and pollen, young bees and even beeswax. Bears, badgers and bee-eater birds tear into the nest to eat the contents. Some insects, such as waxmoths, are specialized to feed on particular bee products, including, as their name suggests, wax.

Bees try to defend the nest with their stings, but may not manage to fight off their enemies. Wasp, ant and termite nests contain large numbers of only young insects, but they provide a good meal.

▲ **FOREST FEAST**
Silky anteaters live in the forests of Central and South America. They feed on forest-dwelling ants and termites. Like other mammals that eat ants, they have long snouts, sticky tongues and sharp claws.

▲ **GRASSLAND ANTEATER**
This giant anteater is probing a termite mound with its long, sticky tongue. These bushy-tailed mammals, which live in Central and South American grasslands, are major enemies of ants and termites.

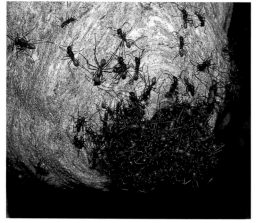

▲ **INVASION FORCE**
These army ants are invading a wasps' nest. They will break into the wasps' nest to steal – and later feast on – the young wasps. Army ants are enemies of many social insects, including other types of ants and termites.

◄ FOLLOW THE BIRD

This bird is a honey guide, and it is found in Africa and western Asia. Its favorite foods are found in bees' nests. It can't attack a nest by itself, so it enlists the help of a mammal called a honey badger, or ratel. The honey guide makes a special call and the badger follows the bird to the bee's nest. The ratel breaks open the nest to get to the honey, allowing the bird to feed on the bee larvae, the wax and the remains of the honey. Honey guides also lead people to bees' nests for the same reason.

BLOOD-SUCKING PARASITE ►

One of a bee colony's worst enemies is a tiny creature called the varroa mite. This photograph of the mite has been magnified many times. This eight-legged creature lives on the bee's skin and sucks its blood. Some varroa mites carry disease. Another type of mite, the tracheal mite, infests the bee's breathing tubes. The two types of mites have destroyed thousands of bee colonies worldwide in the last ten years.

◄ EATEN ALIVE

This solitary wasp, called a bee-killer, has captured and paralyzed a worker bee and is dragging it to its burrow. In the burrow, the bee-killer wasp will lay an egg on the unlucky worker. When the young wasp larva hatches out, it feeds on the still-living bee, and so the bee becomes food for the wasp's young.

Solitary Relatives

Bees, wasps, ants and termites are the only types of insects that include truly social species. However, many types of bees and wasps are solitary, and do not rear their own young.

leafcutter bee
(*Megachile* species)

After mating, the female lays her eggs, often in a specially prepared nest stocked with food for the babies. Solitary wasps provide insect prey for their young to feed on. Solitary bees lay in a store of bee-bread, which is a mixture of nectar and pollen. Then the female flies away and takes no further care of her young.

In the wider world of insects, a few other species show some social behavior. Female earwigs tend their eggs, and shield bugs stay with their young and guard them from enemies. However, they are not truly social because they do not work together to raise their young, or have castes that perform different tasks in the colony.

◄ **PREPARING THE NEST**
This leafcutter bee is carrying a piece of leaf to her nest. Solitary bees, such as this one, build underground nests for their young. They line the nests with pieces of leaf or petal that they snip off with their scissor-like jaws.

▲ **STOCKING UP**
This potter wasp has paralyzed a caterpillar and is dragging it back to the nest for its young to feed on when it hatches. This solitary wasp gets its name from the pot-shaped nests it molds from clay.

◄ **PARASITIC WASPS**
Braconid wasp larvae emerge from a hawkmoth caterpillar when they are ready to pupate. This family of wasps builds no nests for their young. Instead, they lay their eggs in slow-moving insects such as caterpillars. When the eggs hatch, the larvae feast off their host as parasites.

HIBERNATING IN CLUSTERS ▶

Monarch butterflies show some signs of social behavior. They have gathered in a flock to hibernate on a sheltered tree. In autumn, monarch butterflies fly hundreds of miles south to spend the winter in warmer countries. In spring, they fly north again to lay their eggs.

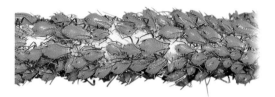

▲ GROUP FEEDERS

In summer, rose aphids gather on the stems and leaves of garden plants to suck juicy plant sap. The insects may collect together on their favorite food plants, but do not actively cooperate with one another, and so are not classed as social.

field digger wasp
(*Mellinus arvensis*)

◀ TAKEOUT SUPPER

This field digger wasp is carrying a captured fly to her underground burrow, where it will feed her young. Instead of stinging their victims, some types of solitary wasps bite their prey to subdue them, before using them to stock their nests.

Did you know? Some solitary mason bees build clay nests on walls, or lay their eggs in abandoned snail shells.

INSECT SWARMS ▶

Locusts are relatives of grasshoppers and live mostly in hot, dry countries. During the long, dry season, locusts are solitary, but when rain falls and plants flourish, they gather and breed quickly to form large swarms. The adult locusts gather in huge, destructive swarms and fly around the countryside looking for food.

How Insects Evolved

Insects are a very ancient group of creatures. They started to evolve from common ancestors about 400 million years ago and developed into about 30 or so orders (types). Insects were the first creatures to fly, and some evolved wings more than 350 million years ago.

Relatively few fossils of prehistoric insects survive because insects are so small and fragile. However, some fossils have been preserved in amber (hardened tree resin). Experts believe that modern ants, wasps and bees all evolved from the same wasp-like, meat-eating ancestors.

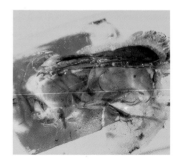

▲ FOSSILIZED IN AMBER
This prehistoric bee has been preserved in amber. About 40–50 million years ago, the bee landed on the trunk of a pine tree and became trapped in the sticky resin. Later, the resin slowly hardened to become clear, golden-colored amber, which is often used to make jewelry.

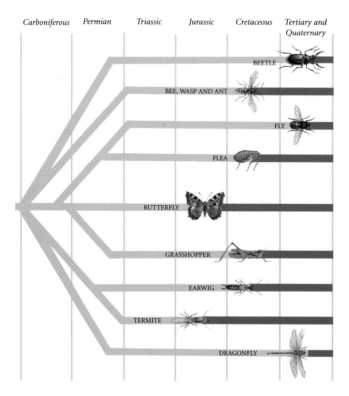

◄ INSECT EVOLUTION
This diagram shows the time period when some insect orders evolved and how they are related to each other. There are more than a million different insect species divided into about 30 orders. Bees, wasps and ants belong to the order Hymenoptera. Termites belong to a separate order, Isoptera. As this diagram shows, termites developed earlier than many other insects. They are more closely related to earwigs than they are to bees, wasps and ants.

◄ ANCIENT TERMITE

This winged male termite became trapped in tree resin about 30 million years ago. As you can see, the insect's delicate wings, legs and even its antennae have been preserved in the amber. The oldest amber fossils date back to about 100 million years ago, but termites are thought to have evolved long before that.

A NEW PARTNERSHIP ►

The ancestors of bees and wasps were meat-eaters. About 100 million years ago, bees began to feed on pollen and nectar from newly evolved flowers. Experts think that plants developed the flowers to lure insects into helping them with pollination. The partnership between insects and flowering plants flourished, and the number of both species increased greatly.

brown bumblebee
(*Bombus pascuorum*)

▲ TERROR OF THE PAST

About 45 million years ago, giant ants roamed the forests of Europe. This picture shows how a worker may have looked. The ants probably lived in large colonies and were carnivorous, just like many ants today. The queens were the largest ants ever to have lived and had a wing-span of up to 5 inches, which is larger than some hummingbirds.

▲ PREHISTORIC HUNTER

This amber fossil contains an ant with two mosquito-like insects. The ant, a meat-eating hunter, became trapped in the resin while preying on one of the mosquitoes. Its leg can still be seen between the ant's jaws. Experts believe ants were originally ground-dwelling insects. Later they became social and began to live in underground nests.

Insect Societies and People

Social insects affect our lives and the world we live in. We think of some species as friends, others as enemies. Bees are important because they pollinate crops and wild plants. They also give us honey and many other products. We fear bees and wasps for their stings, which can kill if the victim has a strong allergic reaction. However, bee venom contains chemicals that are used in medicine. Wasps help us by killing huge numbers of pests that feed on farmers' crops.

Plant-eating ants damage gardens and orchards, and can spoil food stores. Some types of ants protect aphids, which are a pest in gardens, but other ants hunt and kill crop-harming pests. In tropical countries, termites cause great damage in farm fields and orchards and to wooden houses. However, even termites play an important role in the cycle of life in their natural habitats.

▲ **WONDERFUL WAX**
Bees do not just give us honey – they also produce beeswax, which is used to make polish and candles, like the ones shown here. People eat pollen pellets collected by bees, and royal jelly, which young bees feed on, because they are healthy and nourishing.

Did you know? In Australia, Aboriginals eat honeypot ants like candy.

◀ **WASP SAVES CABBAGE**
This hornet is eating a cabbage white caterpillar, which feeds on cabbage plants and is a pest for farmers and gardeners. Hornets are among the many wasp species that help farmers and gardeners by killing large numbers of insects that harm crops and plants. Other, solitary, species of wasps specialize in preying on aphids, caterpillars and other pests.

▲ PLANTATION PEST

In warm countries, leafcutter ants can become a major pest in farm fields and orchards. These insects need large quantities of leaves to feed the fungi in their fungus gardens. A large colony of leafcutters can strip a fruit tree bare of leaves in a single night.

▲ PROTECTING THE TREES

These weaver ants are being used to control pests in an orange orchard. In China, weaver ant nests have been sold for the last 2,000 years, making them the earliest-known form of natural pest control. Farmers hang the nests in their trees and the ants eat the harmful pests.

◄ EATING SOCIAL INSECTS

This man from West Africa is eating a fat, juicy termite queen, which is considered to be a delicacy in that part of the world. Social insects, including adult termites and young wasps, bees and ants, are eaten in many parts of the world, including Australia. In Western countries, people are squeamish about eating insects, but in some developing countries, tasty and nourishing insects provide up to 10 percent of the animal protein in people's diets.

READ ALL ABOUT TERMITE DAMAGE ▶

Wood-eating termites have damaged this book. Termites also cause major damage to timber structures in some parts of the world. Some species burrow under buildings, where they damage the wooden foundations. People often do not even know the termites are there until the damage is done and the wood is eaten away. Termites also cause havoc by eating wooden ties used on railway tracks.

Collecting Honey

People have eaten honey as a natural delicacy since the beginning of human history. Long before written records existed, people raided wild bees' nests to harvest this sweet food. A prehistoric cave painting dating to 7000BC shows a person taking honeycomb from a bees' nest. About 3,000 years ago, people began to domesticate bees and keep them in hives so they could harvest the honey more easily. Beekeeping is now practiced throughout the world.

Several different species of honeybee exist; the best known is the European honeybee, which produces large amounts of honey. This bee, originally from the Middle East and Asia, colonized Europe long ago, and was later taken to North America by early settlers. Now it is found on every continent except Antarctica.

TRADITIONAL HIVES
This photo, taken around 1900, shows traditional methods of beekeeping. In past centuries, honeybees were kept in straw containers called skeps, shown here. This brave beekeeper has no protective clothing for her arms and head.

A MODERN HOME
Most beehives are wooden boxes containing several frames. The upper boxes of frames can be removed, allowing the beekeeper to reach the bees and honey. The queen and her brood live in the lower frames. The workers store nectar and pollen in the upper boxes of frames, called supers. The beekeeper harvests honey from the supers. A metal screen prevents the queen from laying eggs in the supers.

from Bees

THE BUSINESS OF POLLINATION

This field of sunflowers has been pollinated by bees. In North America and Australia, beekeeping is big business. Farmers and orchard owners hire the bees to pollinate their crops. Beekeepers travel thousands of miles to move their bees to regions where plants are flowering and producing nectar. Many beekeeping businesses are run by local farmers. Others are owned by large corporations.

DIFFICULT ACCESS

In the mountain kingdom of Nepal in Asia, giant Himalayan honeybees nest in caves and cracks in vertical cliff faces. These bees are adapted to survive in the cold mountain climate. Local people risk their lives to reach the honey.

COVERING UP

Modern beekeepers wear protective clothing. Nylon overalls, gloves, thick boots and a hat with a veil help protect the wearer from stings. Keepers may also pacify their bees with smoke, but they still get stung frequently.

59

Conservation

Just as social insects affect our lives, so we affect the lives of social insects. As human populations expand, we change the wild places where insects live. For example, large areas of tropical rainforest are being felled for timber or fuel, and to build settlements. This threatens the survival of the forest's plants and animals, including social insects. In developed countries all over the world, farms cover large areas that used to be wild. Crops are a feast for some insect pests, so their numbers multiply quickly. Many farmers use chemical insecticides to protect their crops from the pests, but these chemicals kill 'beneficial' insects along with the pests.

All over the world, conservationists fight to save rare animal species, such as tigers. It is important that we start to protect social insects, too.

▲ POISON SPRAY
A tractor sprays insecticide over a field. The poisonous chemicals kill not only pests but also other insects such as bees, which pollinate flowers, and wasps, which prey on the pests. Some types of insecticide are now banned because they damage and pollute the natural world. Herbicides designed to control weeds also kill wild plants that social insects feed on.

◄ FOREST DESTRUCTION
A forest is being felled for timber. The tropical rainforests contain over half of all known animal species, including thousands of social insects. Destroying forests affects not only large animals but also tiny insects. Experts fear that some social insects in these huge forests may become extinct before they have even been identified.

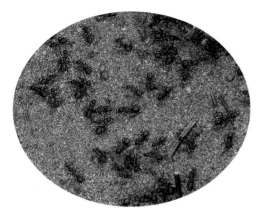

◄ PROTECTED BY LAW

In temperate forests, wood ant colonies do a vital job in preying on insects that harm the forest. In Aachen, Germany, in 1880, the wood ant became the first insect to be protected by a conservation law. It is now protected in several other European countries. Foresters also help to protect the insects by screening off their mounds to prevent people from stealing the young ants to use as fish food. Although one wood ants' nest may contain up to a million insects, including several hundred queens, it is still vulnerable to human destruction.

HELPING THE FOREST ►

Termites become our enemies when they move into our houses and eat wooden beams and furniture. People kill them using poisonous chemicals. In the wild, however, even these unpopular insects do a useful job. As they munch through leaves and wood, they help to break down plant matter so the goodness it contains returns to fertilize the soil.

◄ RARE BEE

A long-tongued bumblebee feeds from a field bean flower. This and several other crops can be pollinated only by bumblebees with long tongues. In some areas, however, domestic honeybees now thrive at the expense of the native long-tongued bees. When the long-tongued bees become scarce, the plants that depend on them for pollination are threatened too.

VITAL FOR POLLINATION ►

Many of our most popular fruits, vegetables and other crops are pollinated by honeybees. These include apples, pears, melons, onions, carrots, turnips and cotton. Experts estimate that up to a third of all human foods depend on bees for pollination.

GLOSSARY

abdomen
The rear part of an insect's body. This section contains the reproductive organs and part of the digestive system.

amber
A type of fossilized tree resin, often used to make jewelry.

antenna (pl. antennae)
The long projections on an insect's head, which it uses to smell, touch and taste.

brood cells
The cells inside a bees' or wasps' nest in which the young insects grow.

caste
A particular type of insect within a colony, which performs certain special tasks.

cells
The six-sided containers inside a bees' or wasps' nest, in which the young insects grow and where bees also store food.

colony
A large group of insects that live together.

comb
The flat sheets inside a bees' or wasps' nest made up of hundreds of cells joined together.

compound eyes
The large eyes found on wasps, bees and other insects, which have many lenses.

crop
A part of the digestive system that some insects use to store food. The honey stomach.

drone
A male bee.

evolve
An animal species is said to evolve when it changes gradually, over generations, becoming better suited to the conditions in which it lives.

exoskeleton
The hard outer skin of an insect that protects the soft parts inside.

extinct
An animal or plant species is said to be extinct when it dies out completely.

fertile
Able to reproduce. In social insects, the only fertile female is the queen.

fossil
The preserved remains of an animal or its prints, often found in rock but also in amber.

gland
An organ in an animal's body that produces a substance, often a liquid, that has a particular use.

grub
The legless larva of an insect such as a wasp or bee.

habitat
The particular place in which an animal species lives, such as a rainforest or a desert.

honeydew
A sweet fluid given off by sap-sucking insects such as aphids, and eaten by some types of ants.

honey stomach
The organ in a honeybee's body where nectar is stored. The crop.

king
The fertile male termite who lives with the termite queen and fertilizes her eggs.

larva (pl. larvae)
The young of insects such as bees, ants and wasps, which undergo complete metamorphosis.

life cycle
A series of stages in the lives of animals such as insects, as they grow up and become adults.

malpighian tubes
Tubes leading into the junction of an insect's mid and hind gut, involved in urine formation.

mandibles
A pair of jaws at the sides of an insect's mouth, which are used for biting and cutting.

metamorphosis
The transformation of a young insect into an adult. Bees, ants and wasps have a four-stage life cycle – egg, larva, pupa and adult. They are said to exhibit complete metamorphosis. Termites have a three-stage cycle – egg, nymph and adult. They are said to exhibit incomplete metamorphosis.

nectar
A sweet liquid found in flowers that is eaten by insects such as wasps and bees. Plants produce nectar to encourage insects to visit the flower and pollinate it.

nymph
The young of insects, such as termites, that undergo incomplete metamorphosis.

order
A scientific category describing a group of animals with a range of shared characteristics. Ants, wasps and bees make up the insect order Hymenoptera. Termites belong to the insect order Isoptera.

palps
Short feelers on an insect's mouth that help it to find food and guide it into the mouth.

parasite
An animal that lives on or inside another animal and lives off it, sometimes killing it.

pheromones
Special scents given off by animals, such as insects, at certain times to communicate with others of their species.

pollen
The dust-like yellow powder produced by plants. Bees use pollen, together with honey or nectar, to feed their larvae. When they collect pollen, bees fertilize flowers in a process called pollination.

pollination
The transfer of pollen from the male part of a flower to the female part, so that the plant can be fertilized and produce seeds.

predator
An animal that hunts other animals for food.

prey
An animal that is hunted and eaten by a predator.

propolis
A sticky tree resin used by worker honeybees to repair cracks in their nest. It is also known as 'bee glue.'

pupa (pl. pupae)
The third stage in the lives of insects such as wasps, ants and bees before they become adults.

queen
A fertile female insect within a social insect colony, whose job is to lay eggs.

simple eyes
The small, bead-like eyes possessed by insects such as wasps, which can detect the level of light.

social
Living with others of its species in a cooperative group. The colonies of social insects contain different castes and at least two generations. All the insects help to rear the colony's young.

soldier
A caste of insects within a social insect colony, whose job is to defend their nestmates and the nest.

species
A group of animals or plants that share similar characteristics and can breed together to produce fertile young.

spiracles
The tiny holes in an insect's exoskeleton that allow it to breathe.

thorax
The middle section of an insect's body to which the wings and legs are attached.

worker
A nonbreeding insect in a social insect colony who performs many tasks for the group.

INDEX

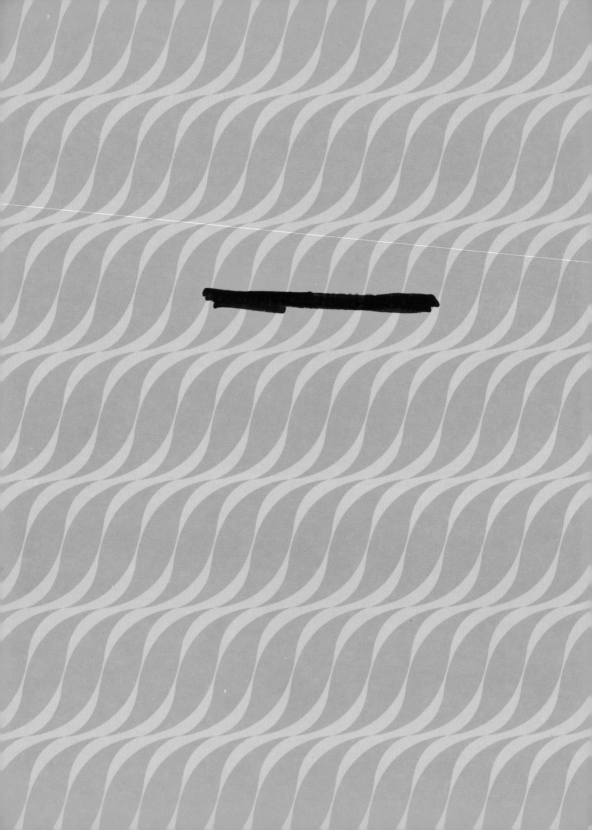